Brat Packs

Magic School

By Deri Robins

illustrated by Martin Chatterton

Hippo

Scholastic Children's Books,
Commonwealth House, 1-19 New Oxford Street
London WC1A 1NU, UK

A division of Scholastic Ltd
London ~ New York ~ Toronto ~ Sydney ~ Auckland
Mexico City ~ New Delhi ~ Hong Kong

Published in the UK by Scholastic Ltd, 2000

Text copyright © Deri Robins, 2000
Illustrations copyright © Martin Chatterton, 2000

ISBN 0 439 99887 5

All rights reserved
Printed by Cox & Wyman

2 4 6 8 10 9 7 5 3 1

Contents

Welcome to Magic School!

Magic School is the coolest school around. Unlike most ordinary schools, there are NO boring lessons, NO sarcastic teachers, and NO stick-out-your-tongue-awful school dinners to spoil your day.

That's the good news.

The bad news is (and maybe you should sit down before you read this):
THERE WILL BE SOME HOMEWORK.
None of our magic lessons are difficult, but the difference between being a grade-A magician and the school dunce comes down to one well-worn little phrase: *practise makes perfect*. It'll be well worth the effort, believe us.
Because once you've got the magic bug, there'll be no stopping you. News of your amazing powers will spread, and people will start treating you with new-found respect. Before you know it, you'll have your own TV show, a yacht in the Caribbean, and more invitations to celebrity parties than you can handle!

So let's get started!

Get your kit on

We can't help noticing that some pupils have arrived without the full kit. These pages are for those of you who still need to get your hat, wand and uniform.

Magic cloak

Cloaks are essential. Apart from the fact that you won't look particularly magical without one, they're wicked for concealing all kinds of secret stuff (more of that later).

To make a cloak, just cut open a black bin-bag, and neaten the edges with scissors.

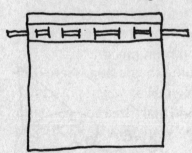

Put some sticky tape along one long edge, about 2 cm down from the top. Cut slits in the tape, then thread with ribbon as shown.

Cut stars and moons from shiny paper, and glue them to the cloak.

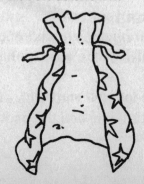

Magician's hat

You'll need to copy these patterns onto some thick black paper.

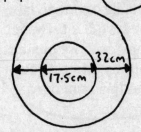

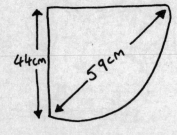

Cut them both out, then roll the triangular piece into a cone. Glue the sides together, and hold them in place with pieces of sticky tape (do this on the inside of the cone).

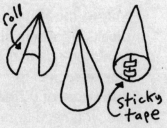

Cut flaps around the base, and fold these up. Glue these flaps to the underneath of the brim piece.

Stick on plenty of glitzy magical shapes, as you did with the cloak.

Wand

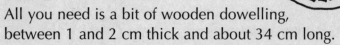

All you need is a bit of wooden dowelling, between 1 and 2 cm thick and about 34 cm long.

Smooth the ends with sandpaper, then paint the ends white and the middle black.

Acting the part

To be an ace magician you need to be an ace performer. How you decide to play it is up to you – you can be cool and nonchalant, or flamboyant and over-the-top – but all the time you need to be acting your socks off…

Here are some essential tips for putting on a blinding magical performance:

❖ Misdirection

If you're doing something tricky with your left hand, you need to *misdirect* your audience's attention to your right hand (and the other way around).

Let's say you're sneakily working a coin down your sleeve and into your hand (see **Now you see it** on page 26). This hand is the last thing you want your audience to be focusing on, so *make* them look at your other hand – wave your wand around, point at something – anything at all to *misdirect* their attention.

❖ Work on your patter

Not only does a lively stream of chat make your performance more interesting, but it helps to distract your audience from all those little tricks and cheats.

Your patter can be slick and funny, or mysterious and wizard-like. Practise it until it sounds natural.

❖ Practise your magic

We can't go on about this often enough. Choose the tricks you're really good at, and practise them until they're as natural to you as breathing.

❖ Be prepared

Memorize the order of the tricks you're going to perform. Check you have all the props you need before you start your display, and make sure they're exactly where you need them.

❖ Quick, slow, quick quick slow

Choose something quick and slick as an opener. Then alternate quick tricks with slightly longer ones, to vary the pace.

❖ Never repeat, never explain

Never repeat a trick, even if your audience begs with tears in their eyes. They'll be watching a whole lot more carefully the second time, and are more likely to rumble you. And never, *ever* explain a trick.

❖ Quit when you're ahead

You should always leave your audience wanting more. Keep your performance short – five or six tricks is about right – and always end with a big finish.

Lesson 1: Conjuring with Cards

OK. Gather round, and stop fiddling with your wands.

Those of you who've been paying attention will have noticed that this book came with a pack of playing cards. These may look perfectly innocent to you – indeed, in the hands of a non-magical person that's exactly what they are. However, once you've studied the following pages *and done your homework properly*, you'll find that these cards will suddenly take on strange and magical powers...

The disappearing card

Before we go any further, you're going to learn how to make a card disappear and reappear. Carry out the following steps slowly to begin with, then practise until you can do them *mind-blowingly fast*.

1 Hold a playing card between your fingers and thumb, as shown.

2 Now bend your second and third fingers behind the card.

3 Press your first and little fingers against the sides of the card.

4 Straighten out your middle fingers so that they flick the card round to the back of your hand. Raise your arm at the same time, as if you've just chucked the card into the air.

5 Straighten out all your fingers, holding just the edges of the card with your first and little fingers.

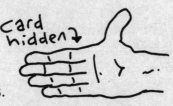

card hidden ↗

To bring the card back, bend all your fingers so that the card flips back into your palm, and hold it between your fingers.

Cartus Disaparecium!

This has absolutely nothing to do with the rest of the feats in this chapter, *but* it's good sleight of hand practice *and* it's a really pukka thing to be able to do.

Pick a card...

This is the most basic card trick of all, but it always looks amazing to a non-magical person. (It's also a wicked way of making extra cash – see opposite).

1 Shuffle the cards, distracting your friends with some lively chat while you do so. Once you've stopped shuffling, take a sneaky glance at the bottom card in the pack. This card is your *key card*.

The rest is laughably easy.

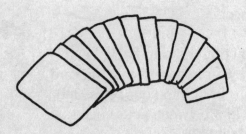

2 Fan out the cards, and ask someone to pick and memorize a card without you seeing it. Ask them to put this card on top of the pile.

3 Cut the pack, and place the bottom pile on the top one. Cut the pack again. By doing this, you have placed your key card on top of your friend's card.

4 Cut the cards again, so that your friend's card seems to be lost in the pack.

5 Deal out the cards face upwards in a fan. Look out for your key card. You know that the card your friend chose is the next one in the pack, so you will have no trouble at all picking it out!

How to double your pocket money

Strictly, of course, we don't approve of this at all at Magic School, and we trust that you won't really try it out on a real live adult.

As if!

As well as your pack of cards, you'll need a non-magical grown-up.

a non-magical grown up →

1 Perform stages 1 to 3 of **Pick a card**.

2 Start dealing out the cards. When you get to your key card, start to look a bit hesitant. Deal out the next card. You know perfectly well that this is the card your non-magical grown-up chose, but *let it go*.

3 Deal out another card, then ask your grown-up if that was the one they chose. When they say no, look a bit confused. Look thoughtful for a bit, then say you know where you've gone wrong.

4 Tell your grown-up that the next card you turn over will be the card they chose. Say you're so certain about this that you'll bet next week's pocket money on it.

5 Once they agree, go back to the correct card – and flip it over!

Tell your friends that you're thinking of trading in your pack of cards, since the royals are getting a bit above themselves. Take the jack of spades, for example, who always insists on jumping to the top of the pile whatever you do…

The jumping jack

1 Show your friends the jack of spades. Do *not* show them the extra card (any one will do) which you have cunningly hidden behind the jack!

2 Place the two cards face down on top of the rest of the pack. Everyone will think that the top card is the jack.

3 Take the top card, and without letting anyone see it, place it in the middle of the pack.

4 Wave your wand over the pack, while muttering suitably magical words.

Cartas Mobilus!

5 Flip over the top card. The jack (which never moved in the first place) is 'back' on top!

15

The wandering queens

And then there's the queens!
You keep trying to split them up,
but they seem to be able to get
back together whatever you do.

1 Show your friends the four queens. As in the
previous trick, you need to conceal extra cards
behind the ones you're showing – in this case,
any other three cards from the pack.

2 Place the seven cards on the top of the pack,
and deal the top four cards as shown:

Your friends will naturally assume that each pile
contains one of the queens.

3 Now deal out the next three cards on top of the
last card. Deal three cards to each of the other
piles in the same way.

4 Invite someone to examine the first pile of cards. No queens! Do the same with the second and third pile. Then flip over the final pile – there they all are, gossiping away as usual!

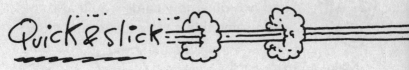

Quick & slick

Hand someone a pack of cards, and invite them to shuffle them for as long as they like. Now take the cards, and hold them behind your back. You can now astound your friends by bringing out the four aces, one by one.

You can carry out this magical feat because you have sensibly removed all the aces before handing over the pack. The aces are held in place with a paper clip, and attached to the inside back of your jacket with a safety pin.

17

The disappearing queen

Having established that the queens are nothing but trouble, you can reveal your plan to put them in their place. You will now show how you can make the queen of spades turn into a lowly two whenever you like!

You'll need the queen of spades from your pack of cards, the two of spades, and two other low cards. You'll also need some thin card, scissors and glue.

Make an extra card from the thin card. Hinge this to the queen of spades with sticky tape, as shown:

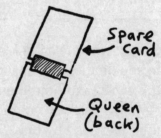

Spare card

Queen (back)

Queen (hinged)

Slip the hinged card over the two of spades, and place it in between the other two cards, so that just the top of the queen is showing.

1 Show this to your friends, then close the cards.

2 Turn the cards over, *so that the hinged piece is nearest to your hand.*

3 Pull out the bottom card, and place it on the table.

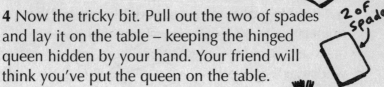

6 of clubs

4 Now the tricky bit. Pull out the two of spades and lay it on the table – keeping the hinged queen hidden by your hand. Your friend will think you've put the queen on the table.

2 of spades

5 Put the last card down, and remind your friend to keep his eye on the queen. While he's looking at the cards, slip the hinged piece into your pocket.

6 Make a big play of moving the cards about, telling your friend to follow the queen. When you've done this for a bit, ask him which one he thinks is the queen.

7 Flip over the other two cards – no-one will be surprised to see they aren't the queen. Then slowly turn over the final card – and find that the queen of spades has become the humble two of spades!

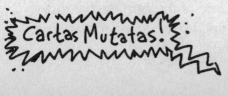

Cartas Mutatas!

The transparent cards

All you need to do is glance at the top card on the pile of cards before you begin. The rest is down to the skill of your performance and sheer nerve.

Let's say the top card's the three of diamonds.

1 Ask a friend to cut the pack into three more or less equal piles. Make sure you keep track of the top third, which contains the three of diamonds (pile *c*).

2 Tell your friend that because you have amazing X-ray vision, you will now be able to identify the top card on each of the three piles.

3 Let your fingers hover over pile *a* – but call out "three of diamonds" nevertheless! Pick the top card up, look at it, but don't let anyone else see it.

4 Then call out the name of the card you've just picked up, while picking up the top card of pile *b*.

5 Finally, call out the name of the second card you picked up, while picking up the three of diamonds from pile c.

6 Toss the cards on to the table, and prove you were right each time!

Wow!

So called because this is the reaction you will get when you pull off this amazing (and completely foolproof) piece of magic.

1 Deal three cards face up on the table, as if you were dealing to three players. Keep dealing the cards, one at a time to each pile, until each pile has seven cards altogether, then put the rest of the pack to one side.

2 Ask your friend to choose any card, and to remember it. All they have to do is tell you which pile their card is in.

3 Now pick up the three piles, and put them one on top of the other – with the pile your friend has pointed to in the middle.

4 Repeat steps 1 to 3 two more times.

5 Now deal out the top ten cards from the pack. Flip over the eleventh card – it's the one your friend chose!

Don't worry about the way this one works. It just does.

The leaping card

If you're going to perform a series of card feats, this makes a suitably dramatic finale.

As well as a normal pack of cards, you'll need a couple of spare ones*, scissors, a pencil and a short piece of elastic (you could cut up a thin elastic band).
*(You could use ordinary card to make spare playing cards, but they will be harder to hide when you're shuffling the cards.)

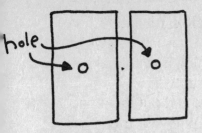

hole

Prepare the spare cards by making a hole in the middle of each one with the pencil. Thread through the elastic, and knot tightly to hold in place.

The piece of elastic in the middle should be just long enough to stretch like this when a card is pushed between them:

side view

1 Put the trick cards at the bottom of the pile, and hide the elastic with your hand. Fan out the pack so that your friend can choose a card.

2 Cut the pack, so that your trick cards are now in the middle. Ask your friend to give you the card she has chosen, and push it in between the two trick cards.

3 Hold the cards firmly in place for a minute or so while you give your friend some old chat. Then, after giving the pack a quick tap with your wand, just loosen your grip so that the card leaps out.

Expelliarmus!

LESSON 2: MAGIC MONEY

Your first lesson will be learning how to make a coin disappear and reappear at will.

The disappearing coin

If you're left-handed, just swop 'right hand' for 'left hand' (and vice versa) whenever you see these instructions in the book).

1 Hold a coin in your left hand, as shown.

2 Now pretend you're going to take the coin with your right hand. Move your right thumb under the coin, and close your right fingers over the coin.

3 Pretend to grab the coin with your right hand, but secretly let it drop into your left palm. Grip the coin lightly between your bent second and third fingers.

Coin is actually here

This is called PALMING.

4 Close your right
hand into a fist,
and move it away.

5 Slowly open
your right hand –
no coin!

Cuneus Disaparecium!

You can now make the coin
reappear from wherever you like.

Coo!

Now all you have to do is
PRACTISE until you can do this in your sleep…

❖ *Tip: try keeping a coin palmed in your hand for
an entire day, until it feels completely natural.*

OK, class.
You can get
your wands
out now.

Now you see it...

You will need to wear a jacket with an inside pocket (or glue one inside your cloak).

Tuck your wand in the pocket before you begin.

1 Perform steps 1 to 4 of **The disappearing coin**.

2 Tell your friends that you are now going to use your wand to make the coin in your right hand disappear. Then put your left hand (in which, of course, you have secretly palmed the coin) inside your jacket.

3 Before you take out your wand, drop the coin down your right sleeve - but keep your elbow bent so that it doesn't fall out completely.

4 Wave your wand over your right fist, muttering a magic spell.

Cuneus Disaparecium!

Open your hand to show that the coin has vanished.

5 Wave your wand about a bit, announcing that it's brilliant for making things vanish. Then, while everyone's busily watching your left hand, straighten your right arm so that the coin falls into your right hand.

6 Tap your right fist, open your hand – and the coin has magically reappeared.

Cuneus Aparecium!

Quick & slick

You'll need two 2p or 10p coins. Using a mirror, practise holding the two coins like this in your right hand. You need to make sure that the horizontal coin is completely hidden from view.

When you're ready, hold up your right hand to show that you're only holding one coin. Wave your left hand round a bit to prove that it's empty. Bring your hands together quickly and separate them – with a coin in each hand!

The wizard's hat

You'll need a glass tumbler, some thin card, some fairly thick coloured paper, scissors and glue.

First, make a tiny wizard's hat. (Use the method shown on page 6, but make the hat just big enough to cover the tumbler.)

Put a little glue all round the rim of the tumbler, and press it down on the paper. When it's dry, trim around the paper *very carefully* with scissors.

Place the tumbler and the hat on another piece of coloured paper (identical to the one used to cover the tumbler).

1 Point out that there is clearly nothing inside the glass. Then borrow a 1p coin, and put it on the paper.

2 Pick up the magic hat, and show it around. Put it over the glass, and lift them both over the coin.

28

3 Wave your wand over the hat, then lift the hat off the glass. The coin (which is neatly hidden under the circle of paper) has totally disappeared.

If you can't work out how to make it magically reappear again, you may as well give up magic and take up woodwork instead.

Wizard's gold

It's a well-known fact that a magic wand can make money double in value immediately.

You'll need a small rectangle of thick paper, sticky tape, scissors, a plate, a cardboard box and ten coins of the same value.

Before you begin, fold the paper in half. Stick three sides of the paper (including the folded edge) to the underside of the plate with sticky tape, to make a pocket.

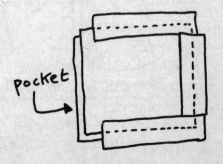

pocket

Put five coins inside
the pocket, then put
the plate on a table.

1 Put the other five coins on the plate, and
announce that you are going to make them
double in value by waving your wand.

2 Show that the box is
empty (hand it round,
if you like). Pick up the
plate, pressing your
fingers over the open
end of the the pocket.

3 Tip the plate into the box so that the coins on
top of the plate *and* the coins in the pocket fall in.
Make sure the pocket can't be seen by anyone as
you do this.

4 Put the plate back down, give the box a
satisfying shake, and tip all ten coins back onto
the plate.

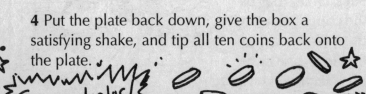

Coneus duplos!

Quick and slick

Although this isn't strictly magic, it will make you look much smarter than everyone else. Which can't be bad.

Fill a glass of water to the very brim, and ask your friends how many coins they think you can put in without the water spilling over.

When they make their guess – which is bound to be far too low – amaze them by sliding dozens and dozens of coins down the inner side of the glass. The water will rise – but if you do it properly, the surface tension will stop it spilling over.

31

LESSON 3: MIND GAMES

Explain to your friends that you have limitless control over what they laughingly call their minds.

Your supreme power

Prove to a friend that you can force her to choose the ace of spades from the pack by magic. Resistance is useless!

Before you begin, arrange the pack so that the ace of spades is the ninth card from the top.

1 Place the cards face down, and ask your friend to pick any number between 10 and 20.

2 Let's say your friend chooses number 14. Remind her that she chose this number of her own free will (or so she imagines), then ask her to count out 14 cards from the top.

3 Now tell her you're going to add the two digits of the number together – in this case, one and four, making five. Take the pile of cards you have dealt, and deal five cards from the top.

4 Ask your friend to turn over the next card. It's the ace of spades.

Conjuring with colour

Here's another way to prove to your friends that their minds are putty in your hands.

You'll need a playing card, a sheet of thin card, felt-tips and scissors.

Draw around the playing card on to the thin card six times. Cut out the cards.

In the top left corner of each card, draw a different shape with felt-tips. Then draw a red circle in the bottom right of each card.

red circle

1 Hold the cards in a fan, with the six different-coloured circles in the top left corners. Show the cards to your friend, making sure that the red circle at the bottom of the top card is hidden by your thumb.

33

2 Explain to your friend that he is powerless to choose any but the card with the red circle. Close up the cards, and turn them in your hand so that all the red circles are now in the top left corners. Distract your friend with misdirection and patter so that he doesn't notice this happening.

3 Shuffle the cards, and fan them out with the backs facing your friend.

4 Ask your friend to pick a card. Take it out of the fan and turn it over, keeping your thumb over the coloured dot at the bottom.

Since he had absolutely no choice in the matter, your friend has of course chosen the card with the red circle.

Mind reading

Since you can control your friend's mind at will, you will obviously have no problem at all when it comes to predicting his thoughts. For this trick you will need the help of a really magic rock band.

Find a picture of your favourite band, and cut out the faces of the various members. (You only need four faces, so chuck any others in the bin.)

You'll also need a small piece of card, an envelope and your magic wand.

On the back of one of the cut-outs, write "you chose me".

On the back of the piece of card, write "you chose...." (writing the name of another member).

Write another band member's name on the front of the envelope.

Finally, write the fourth member's name on a tiny strip of paper, and stick this to the side of your wand.

Put the four cuttings and the piece of card in the envelope. Place it on a table with the front facing down.

1 Take the four cuttings out of the envelope, and put them facing up on the table. Don't let anyone see the writing on the back of the one cutting, *or* the fact that there's a piece of card left in the envelope, *or* the tiny sticker on your wand.

2 Ask your friend to name a band member.

3 Now prove that you knew which member they were going to choose before they did.

If they chose the band member whose name is written on the back, wave your wand and flip it over. Turn over the others too, to prove that only one has writing on the back.

If they chose the band member whose name is on the back of the envelope, wave your wand over this and turn it over.

If they chose the member whose name is on the card, invite them to take this out of the envelope.

If they chose the member named on the wand, wave it in the air a few times and then hold it out for your friend's inspection!

Magical maths

We know what you're thinking. Maths wasn't exactly what you had in mind when you bought this book. However, in this case, it's your friend who'll be doing all the hard multiplication and subtraction, while you sit back and doodle on a piece of paper.

Tell your friend to pick any number smaller than 10.

Ask her to multiply her number by 9.

(While she's taxing her brain to find the answer,
start doodling a big number 6 on a pad of paper.
Don't let anyone see what you're up to.)

Tell your friend to add the two digits of her answer
together, then to add 9 to her total number. She
should then divide this figure by 3.

Ask your friend which number she ended up with
(it will *always* be 6), and as she opens her mouth,
flip the pad of paper around to show that you
knew the answer all along.

You've got thought mail

For this feat, you're going to need a magical apprentice. A fairly intelligent brother or sister would be ideal (are we asking too much?), since they'll need to be at home near a telephone while you're performing elsewhere.

Tell everyone in the room that you have amazing thought-transferring powers, and can prove it with the help of a volunteer and a pack of cards. Ask the volunteer (we'll call her Sophie) to pick a card from the pack, and tell you what it is.

Telephone your apprentice (we'll call him Ben). As soon as he picks up the phone, say (as if in an aside to Sophie), "the phone's ringing". This is Ben's cue to slowly recite the four *suits* in a pack of cards:

"Diamonds…hearts…spades…clubs…"

As soon as Ben names the correct suit, interrupt him by saying "Hello, Ben?" If you interrupt him just after he says "diamonds" he will know that this is the suit that Sophie chose (and so on).

38

Carry on by saying something like "Ben, I need you to concentrate for a sec. I'm going to think of a card, and send it to you by thought-transference."

The word 'transference' is Ben's cue to start reeling off the *numbers* in a suit of cards, starting with the one and ending with the ace. Once he's named the correct number, stop him by saying something like: "OK? Ben, can you now tell Sophie which card she has chosen?"

Pass the phone to Sophie. Get ready to catch her when she faints in wonder as Ben correctly names her chosen card.

Unlike most tricks, this is one that you can risk repeating. Just make sure that the dialogue sounds fresh and natural each time you do it.

Traffic lights

You'll need your apprentice in the room with you for this one.

Turn your back, and ask someone to point at an object in the room. When you turn around again, have your apprentice point to several objects, while asking you if this was the one that was chosen. You will know which object was chosen because they always point to something green *before* they point at the correct one!

The next time you do this, they should point at something orange – and the third time it should be something red.

Phoning it in

Agree a number with your trusty apprentice. Your telephone number is a good choice, providing you can both remember it.

Leave the room or turn your back while everyone chooses a person in the room.

If your telephone number starts with a three, the correct person will be the third one your apprentice points to.

The next time you make a guess, your apprentice will use the second number in the code, and so on.

The magic library

Lay nine books in a row, and turn your back. Ask a friend to point silently at one of the books.

When you turn around again, your apprentice will point to a book that was *not* chosen, and ask you if this was the book.

You then astound the rest of the room by saying "no – but I know which one it was!"

You know this because you will have looked *oh so carefully* at the part of the book your apprentice is pointing at.
You have to imagine that the book is divided into nine parts, and that these parts are numbered as shown:

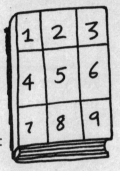

If your apprentice points to the top middle of the book, you need to count *two* books along to find the right one. If he points halfway down the right hand side, it's the *sixth* book – and so on.

❖ *You can try this with any kind of rectangular object – how about grabbing nine greetings cards at Christmas for a 'spontaneous' seasonal trick?*

LESSON 4: DIABOLIC DICE

To perform the feats in this section, you will need
the dice which we have generously provided
in the *Magic School* pack.

The miracle dice

Place the dice in the yellow box, with all the ones
facing towards you (it doesn't matter which
numbers are facing upwards, but they shouldn't
all be the same).

Ask your friends to examine the dice, and tell
them that you will now make all the ones jump to
the top.

Put the lid on, and hold your arm out at a slight
angle, with your thumb and first finger gripping
the box. Jerk the box up and down once, then
open the box.

Datus mutatas!

If you've done it properly –
and you'll need to practise –
you'll find that all the dice
have turned over and all the
ones are now on the top.

42

The rattling die

You'll need two of the dice from this pack, three small empty matchboxes and an elastic band.

Put one of the dice in one of the matchboxes, and strap this to your left arm (near your wrist) with the elastic band. Make sure the box is completely covered by your jacket sleeve.

1 Use your right hand to show everyone the other matchboxes, and prove that they are all empty. *Keep your left hand as still as possible.*

2 Pick up the other die, and *pretend* to drop it in one of the other boxes. Secretly you must palm the die in your right hand, as shown:

3 Transfer this matchbox to your left hand, and give it a good shake. The *hidden* box will make a rattling sound, convincing everyone that the box in your hand really does contain the die.
Slip the other die into a pocket while everyone is busily looking at your left hand!

4 Place the box back on the table, and give it another little shake with your left hand. Rattle! Then take the other box, and shake it with your right hand. No rattle!

5 Move the two boxes around slowly, telling your friends to keep track of 'the box with the die in'. After a while ask someone to tell you where the die is. They should point quite confidently at the box you picked up at the beginning.
Pick up this box with your *right* hand, and give it a good shake. No rattle!

6 Then pick up the other box with your *left* hand, and shake it. Rattle!

7 Do this three more times, until your friends suspect that they have completely lost the plot. After the third time, move the boxes around as before, then pick up the box that they all think contains the die. Give it a reassuring rattle, then put it down again.

8 Reach for your wand with your right hand, and wave it over the box.

Datus disaparacium!

Invite someone to open the box. No die! Ask them to open the other box. No die!!

Bring out the die from your pocket, and wait for the tumultuous applause!

The starry dice

You'll need four of the dice, three napkins or handkerchiefs, some sticky stars (you'll need three different colours – let's say red, silver and gold), and your wand.

Stick a gold star to one of the dice, a silver star to another one, and a red star to each of the two remaining dice.

Put stickers on the napkins too, so that one is starred with red, one with gold and one with silver.

Palm one of the dice with a red star in your right hand (see page 24), and lay the napkins on the table in front of you with the other dice.

1 Explain that you are now going to wrap the die with the gold star in the napkin covered in red stars. Pick these up, so that the napkin is in your left hand, and the die is in your right hand.

2 With your hand hidden behind the napkin, switch the dice around, so that you secretly wrap the die with the red star inside the napkin. The die with the gold star is now palmed in your hand.

45

3 Put this package on the table. Then pick up the napkin with the gold stars and the die with the silver stars, and do exactly the same thing.

4 Finally, pick up the napkin with the gold stars and the die with the red star, and do the same thing. Keep pointing out that none of the dice match the napkins they are wrapped in at present.

5 Whip out your wand, and mutter a spell. Explain that this will cause the three dice to leap into their matching napkins.

Datus mobilus!

Now replace your wand (and the spare die with the red star) in your pocket.

6 Ask someone to open the packages. All three dice have mysteriously changed places, just as you said.

One final mind-blowing dice feat

1 Ask one of your friends to roll three dice while your back is turned. Tell him to add up the numbers on their faces without touching the dice.

2 Now ask him to turn over any two of the dice, and add the bottom numbers to the total figure.

3 Tell him to throw the two dice, and add the two top faces to the total.

4 Now he must take one of the dice, and add the bottom face to the total. Finally, he should throw this die and add the top face to the total.

5 Turn around and look at the dice on the table. In one-point-three milliseconds, you will be able to tell your astounded friend exactly what his total is.

Here's the magical secret: all you need to do is add up the top faces of the dice, and then add 21.

How does it work? Pure magic, of course. We're hurt you asked.

LESSON 5: STRINGS, RINGS (AND OTHER THINGS)

In the right pair of hands, even a ball of string can be a magical thing...

The disappearing ring

You'll need a ring, a large square piece of cloth, a long pencil, a small paper bag (the sort you get from the sweet shop) and your wand.

Sew a hem on all four sides of the piece of cloth – *with the ring trapped inside one of the corners.*

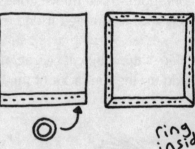

ring inside hem

1 Hold the cloth with the ring between your finger and thumb. Shake it about to show that there's nothing in it, and ask someone if they have a ring you can borrow (have a spare one ready in case they don't).

2 Place the cloth over the ring. Scoop up the cloth with your left hand, tucking in the corners so that the sewn-in ring is near the middle. At the same time, remove the borrowed ring with your right hand.

3 Tell someone to hold the cloth, and ask them if they can feel the ring. Once they've agreed that they can, carefully take the cloth from them, and lay it on the table.

4 Pick up the paper bag with your right hand. Hold the bag with your thumb on the outside, and your fingers inside. The borrowed ring must be between your fingers and the inside of the bag.

5 Hold the bag upside down. Show it around to prove that it's empty.

6 Take the pencil, and push it through the side of the bag. Get the ring on the pencil, then push the point out through the other side of the bag. Fold the top of the bag over, then ask someone to hold the ends of the pencil.

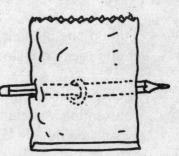

7 Announce that you are now going to make the ring disappear from the hankie. Wave your wand over the hankie, then pick it up and shake it.

Circus disaparecium!

8 Tell the person holding the pencil to hold on very tightly. Grab the bottom of the bag and tug it sharply, so that it's torn right off the pencil.

49

And there on the
pencil, for all to see, is
the ring you borrowed!

Circus aparecium!

The bangle wangle

You'll need a piece of string about 80 cm long,
and two identical bangles. You'll also need to be
wearing a jacket with fairly loose-fitting sleeves
and an inside pocket.

Pull on one of the bangles before you start. Push
it up inside your sleeve so that nobody can see it.

1 Give someone the string and the other bangle
to examine. Ask them to tie the string to your
wrists in a double knot.

2 Ask them to give you the bangle, then spin
around. Pop the loose bangle into your inside
pocket, while pulling the other bangle down so
that it's over the string.

3 Turn around –
astoundingly, you have
threaded the bangle on
to the string without
untying the ends!

The stretching string

You'll need a short piece of string (about 40 cm) and a much longer one (about 2 m). You'll also need a jacket with long sleeves and your wand.

Before you start, pass the longer string up your sleeve, and down inside your jacket or shirt. The end should be just out of view.

1 Hand the short length of string around, and explain that you will transform it into a much longer one. Then fold up the string very tightly and push it into your right fist.

2 Pull out your wand, and wave it over the string.

Increscerium!

3 You now fish out the end of the longer piece of string, and pull it out with a flourish. While your friends are marvelling over this feat, drop the short piece of string into your pocket, with the pretence of replacing your wand. They'll never notice.

Quick and slick

Can you tie a knot in a piece of string without letting go of the ends? Of course you can – provided that you fold your arms before picking up the string! As you unfold your arms, the 'knot' in your arms is magically transported to the knot in the string…

Neat, or what??

One for Harry

We offer this in humble tribute to the famous magician Harry Houdini. Harry was an escapologist – which is just a posh way of saying that he was a whizz at getting out of tight spaces in a hurry.

You'll need a large sack with a long piece of string sewn into the hem at the top.

If you don't have one of these, and you probably don't, get hold of an old sheet, fold it in half and sew it up like this:

Fold sheet in half

Sew up sides

leave gap

tie ends

Warning: *ask permission first, since we know no magic strong enough to disarm an angry parent.*

Make sure that there's a gap in the hem, and pull down a generous loop of string. Tie this in a single knot, and tuck the loose ends back into the hem.

1 Get into the sack, and ask your friends to tie the ends as securely as possible. They will naturally do everything in their power to make sure the ends can't be easily untied.

2 Hop outside the door (or behind a screen made by pinning up yet another old sheet). Pull out the inside knot, and undo the string. You can then wriggle out of the sack quite easily.

3 Make a knot in the loop, so that the bag is closed again. Tuck the knot under the hem. Open the door and reveal that although the bag is still securely tied, you have miraculously escaped!

Pulling power

You'll need a key, a piece of elastic about 30 cm long and a safety pin.

Tie one end of the elastic to the safety pin, and fasten the pin inside the right sleeve of your jacket.

Tie the key to the other end of the elastic, making sure that it's out of sight.

1 Pull the key down and hold it between the fingers and thumb of your right hand. Make sure that no-one can see the elastic.

2 Show that you are placing the key in your left hand. Close your left hand to make a fist. As you do so, just let go of the key so that it whizzes back up your right sleeve.

3 Show that your right hand is empty, then open your left hand. To everyone's amazement, the key has completely vanished.

❖ *You can also do this trick using a silk scarf in place of a key. This tickles.*

54

LESSON 6: GOING PUBLIC

By now, it's time you tried out your magic on a real-life audience. These final offerings will definitely spice up your performance...

The magic scarf

Put a silk scarf around your neck like this. Tuck the front bit under the top of a high-necked T-shirt.

Ask (as casually as you can) if anyone believes in magic, and endure the rude comments that are bound to follow.

Then say, "In that case, presumably you don't believe that I can make this scarf pass right through my neck?"

Then, before your friends can reply, take both ends of the scarf and tug sharply.

Chuck the scarf to one side, and proceed directly to your next trick as if nothing untoward had happened.

Cutting David Beckham in half

You'll need a longish envelope, glue, scissors, and two identical photocopies of your best mate's fave celebrity. The figures should be about 8 cm long.

(If you can't talk anyone into letting you make the photocopies, do your best with a pen and paper)

Seal up the envelope. Cut off both the ends, then cut two slits in the back, about 9 cm apart.

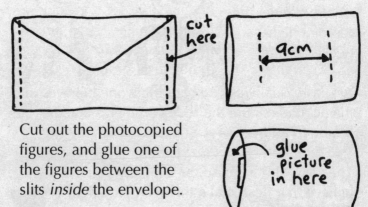

Cut out the photocopied figures, and glue one of the figures between the slits *inside* the envelope.

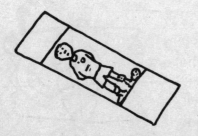

Glue the other figure on to a strip of thin card, which you should be able to slide in and out of the slits.

Place the envelope on the table, with the cut side facing down.

1 Show your mate the strip of card bearing his or her fave celebrity, and break the news that you are about to cut it in half.

2 Pick up the envelope, making sure you keep the cut side towards you. Start pushing the strip of card through the envelope, squeezing the sides slightly. This makes the envelope bow, so that the strip can pass through the slits, as shown.

3 Cut right through the envelope, ignoring any screams of anguish from your mate. Make sure that you slide the blades of the scissors in between the strip and the envelope.

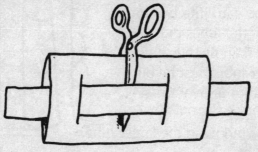

4 Bend the envelope open slightly, proving that the celebrity you stuck to the inside has been cut in half.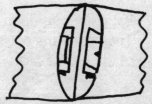

5 Then tell your mate that you have relented, and let them pull the strip. Out comes their fave celebrity – totally unharmed!

The dark arts

If you've always yearned to pull a real live rabbit out of a hat, this one's for you. (OK, there's no hat *as such*, and the bunny's stuffed – but it's the same idea.)

This kind of feat is called 'black art' throughout the magical world, for reasons which will shortly become obvious.

You'll need some fairly stiff thin card, paint (including black paint), a small box, sticky tape and scissors.

Roll the card into two tubes. One of the tubes must be bigger than the other, and the smaller tube must be big enough to fit over the box.

Cut a window in the larger tube.

Window

Paint the outside of the tubes in bright colours. Then paint the outside of the box and the inside of the tubes black.

black

black

58

Put a toy rabbit (or a selection of stuff) inside the black box, and put the box inside the smaller tube. Put the big tube over the top.

black on outside

the box is in here

1 Pick up the outer tube, and show your audience that it is empty. Put it back over the smaller tube.

2 Lift up the inner tube, and show that this is empty too.

box is still in here

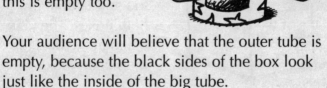

Your audience will believe that the outer tube is empty, because the black sides of the box look just like the inside of the big tube.

3 Put the inner tube back in place. Bring out your rabbit, and wait for the gasps of amazement.

Draw on the dark arts to produce your school report from an empty box! Your parents will be so impressed by this highly amusing feat that they're bound to overlook your dismal grades...

Either of the following would make a fab finale.

Out of the box

You'll need two really
big boxes – the
smallest one must be
large enough for an
assistant to hide in,
and the other one
must be a bit bigger
than that.

flap

Ask a grown-up to
help you cut off the
top and bottom of
both boxes. Then cut
a flap in the back of
the smaller box.

Fold up the boxes, and prop them up so that your
assistant can hide behind them. The smaller one
must be in front, with the flap hidden from view.

FRONT view   BACK view

❖ *Your audience should **sit** so they can't see into the box from the top!*

1 Hold up the small box, keeping the flap at the back. Put it over your head to show that it's empty.

2 Put the box down exactly as shown, so that your assistant can climb through the flap without anyone seeing. Lean casually on top of the box while she is doing this, to stop it wobbling.

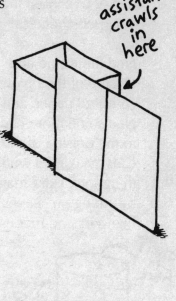

assistant crawls in here

❖ *Tip: it's a good idea to play loud funky music during this trick, to hide any furtive rustling.*

3 Once your assistant is safely inside, pick up the bigger box and show that it's empty. Now place this over the smaller box.

4 At your command, your lovely assistant will amaze your audience by leaping out of the box!

The big finish

For this amazing feat of transfiguration, you'll need a big box, plenty of crepe or tissue paper, and two identical empty tins or canisters. You'll also be thrilled to hear that you'll need a HUGE bag of popcorn, and a handful of colourfully-wrapped choccies!

Line the inside and outside of the box with coloured paper, and glue some more paper to the outside of the cans. Make the whole thing look extra magical by gluing on shapes like stars and moons.

chocs in here

popcorn glued to can

Glue popcorn to the bottom of one of the cans. Fill the can with chocolates, then glue a circle of tissue paper over the open end.

Fill the box with popcorn, and bury the can with the choccies under the surface.

Show everyone the box, and explain that you're going to attempt a very difficult transfiguration exercise.

1 Take the empty can, and use it to scoop up some of the popcorn. Hold up the can and pour the popcorn back into the box. Repeat this two more times.

2 On the fourth dip, leave the ordinary can in the box, and bring out the prepared one. Keep your fingers under the tissue cover to stop it breaking.

3 Cover the can with crepe paper, and use your wand to burst through the cover. The popcorn has magically transformed into choccies!

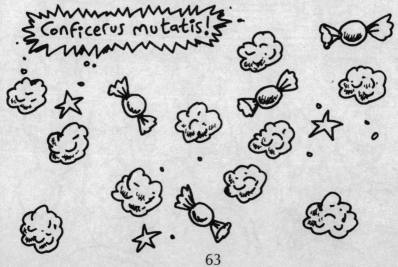

Conficerus mutatis!